The New Year's Goldfish

A Nowruz Story

It was the morning before Nowruz and Keyan could not contain his excitement.

Dad cleaned the entire house, but Keyan accidentally brought mud in with his shoes. Mom picked out new clothes for Keyan and his older sister Leila, but he already ripped the seams. Keyan wanted to help arrange the New Year's spread, but he cracked one of Leila's beautifully decorated eggs.

Now Mom and Leila were busy cooking, and Keyan wondered how he could be helpful.

He remembered the goldfish from their New Year's spread last year. She did a flip in her fish bowl at the exact moment that the year turned. But afterwards they had let that goldfish swim free in the stream in their backyard.

"We still need one very important thing to help us welcome the new year," announced Keyan. "Can I can pick out our Nowruz goldfish this year?"

"That's a wonderful idea!" agreed Leila and Mom.

Keyan was very excited. He was sure he could do an excellent job picking out the very best goldfish to complete his family's New Year's spread.

Keyan and Dad got ready and left the house right away. They walked down the sidewalk, past the busy neighborhood play-ground, and past the bakeries smelling of fresh sweets. They walked past multiple store fronts celebrating spring… until they got to the pet store.

In the back of the pet store they found tanks full of fish. One special goldfish caught Keyan's eye. She swam right up to the side of the tank and seemed to be looking straight at him.

Keyan wasn't sure if she was really looking at him. He stepped to the right, then to the left, then squatted down near the floor. Each time the goldfish followed him. When he stood up, she swam right to the top of the tank... as if to make herself available for catching.

Keyan told Dad and the pet shop owner that this goldfish must be the best one!

The pet shop owner handed Keyan a plastic bag with Goldfish inside of it. Keyan was very happy and wanted to get back home as soon as possible to show Goldfish to Mom and Leila.

Outside the pet shop it was raining. Keyan tucked the bag with Goldfish into his jacket and started walking towards home. But he soon felt a strong flutter from inside his jacket. He took a look and realized Goldfish was splashing her fins in the water.

Again she made intense eye contact with Keyan, which surprised him and he dropped the bag full of water and his fish! The bag broke open and Goldfish swam with the gush of water towards a large puddle in the sidewalk.

Keyan rushed towards Goldfish, but it was raining and the puddles grew with more water. Goldfish continued to swim down the street from puddle to puddle. She swam and Keyan ran after her. From puddle to puddle they made their way down the sidewalk.

Then a group of children saw Keyan running. When they saw the beautiful goldfish he was chasing, they all wanted to catch the fish as well. They jumped in puddles and tried to grab Goldfish... but she was too quick and slippery.

Now Goldfish was swimming towards sewer grates. Keyan was afraid she would fall through the grates and disappear under the ground. Just as she approached the first hole, however, she flipped her body up out of the water and all the way to the other side of the grates.

On the other side of the sewer grates, however, there was not enough water for Goldfish to swim in. The children were catching up to her! Just in time, an older man with a large white beard stepped out the front door of a shop and threw a bucket of water onto the sidewalk. The water splashed onto the sidewalk and carried Goldfish further on down the street.

Now the children were tired and just Keyan was following Goldfish again. The puddles carried Goldfish down a hill. At the bottom of the hill the water and Goldfish joined a stream. The stream was full and the water was running by quickly.

Keyan realized he had followed Goldfish away from the center of town... and away from Dad. He also did not have a goldfish to bring home.

Keyan ran to keep up with Goldfish now swimming happily away in the stream. He could just catch a glimpse of her beautiful red and gold color beneath the water.

Keyan and Goldfish traveled through the backyards of multiple homes, past flowers and fruit trees, and past a field of wild grass.

Finally the water slowed and Goldfish came to the surface. She looked into Keyan's eyes again and her color glistened.

Keyan heard a sound from behind him. He turned and saw Dad jogging towards him. "That was quite an adventure! I didn't know you knew this way back home."

Keyan looked around. Goldfish had found her way to the stream that ran through his very own backyard. She had found a home with fresh water, plenty of food and other friends.

"What a beautiful goldfish!" exclaimed Leila as she came running out of the house with Mom.

In that moment, as Keyan and his family stood together, Goldfish jumped out of the water and did a flip before disappearing again.

Nowruz: The Persian New Year

Nowruz is the most important celebration of the year for many families in the world. Nowruz is most commonly known as the Persian New Year, but people of many countries and many religions celebrate this holiday. The word "Nowruz" means new day. Nowruz starts on the first day of spring (the day of the Spring Equinox), and is celebrated for 13 days.

Khaneh Tekani: Spring Cleaning

The first step in preparing for Nowruz is Khaneh Tekani. "Khaneh" means home and "tekani" means shaking. "Khaneh tekani" means shaking the house… or a really big house cleaning. During Khaneh Tekani, every room in the house is cleaned from top to bottom. After scrubbing and washing everything, families fill their homes with sweet smelling flowers. Each family member also participates in the spring cleaning by buying new clothes to wear on the first day of Nowruz.

Nowruz Sofreh: The New Year Spread

The Nowruz Sofreh is the fancy spread that families put together and then gather around to celebrate Nowruz. The Haft Sin is a collection of seven (haft) items that begin with the Farsi letter "sin". These items are the most important part of the sofreh and represent health, fortune and new beginnings. These are some things that families have on their Haft Sin: sabzeh (sprouts), senjed (fruit of the lotus tree), sib (apple), samanu (wheat pudding), serkeh (vinegar), somaq (sumac), sir (garlic), sekkeh (coins), sonbol (hyacinth flower), sangak (flatbread), or a samovar.

Sabzeh is the most important of the "sin" items on the sofreh. "Sabzeh" means green sprouts. Many people start growing their sprouts weeks before Nowruz. The sprouts are delicate and need a lot of care to grow properly.

In addition to the Haft Sin items, many other things go on the sofreh, including: goldfish, mirrors, candles, decorated eggs, mixed nuts and fruits, rose water, holy books, poetry books, sweets and pastries.

Sal Tahvil: The Strike of the New Year

Sal Tahvil is the exact moment the year turns (when the length of daytime and nighttime are equal). This often falls on March 20th, but can be different every year. Families gather around the sofreh in their new clothes before Sal Tahvil. There is a countdown while everyone closely watches the egg on the mirror and the goldfish in its bowl. There is a legend that says a bullfish in the ocean carries the world on one of its horns. When Sal Tahvil arrives, the bullfish tosses the world to the other horn, causing the world to shake and making the egg roll on the mirror and the goldfish flip over in its water. After the new year arrives, everyone cheers and hugs each other. Older family members give the younger family members Eid-i money and gifts. Everyone celebrates with a large meal.

After the new year arrives, it is time for the younger members of the family to visit the older members of the family and close friends. Many homes are visited. In each home, teas, sweets and fruits are served. These visits continue until the thirteenth day of the new year.

Haji Firouz and Amoo Nowruz

Haji Firouz is the joyful joker who announces that the new year has arrived. He dances, plays instruments and sings songs. He wears a red suit and paints his face with dark make-up. Amoo Nowruz is an older and wiser uncle who keeps track of all of the Nowruz traditions. He also gives gifts to children.

Sizdah Bedar: Thirteenth Day Outing

Sizdah Bedar is the last day of the 13 day Nowruz celebration. "Sizdah" means 13 and "Bedar" means away or out. Thirteen is considered an un-lucky number, so on this day everyone is supposed to leave their homes and have fun outdoors. Families wake up early to pack large picnics and leave for the parks, beaches and country sides. They play games, go on hikes, and eat lots of food all day! Many people also bring the sabzeh from their Haft Sin to throw into a stream. It is unlucky to let the sabzeh turn yellow and die inside your home.

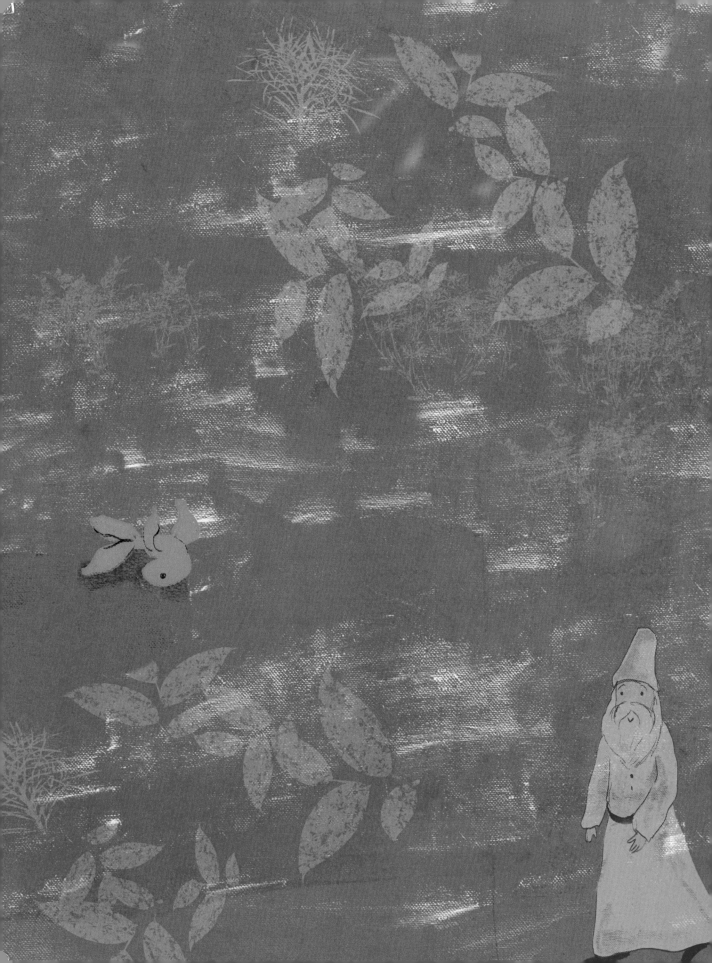

Made in the USA
Middletown, DE
16 March 2018